PAT, THE DOG

Gus Clarke

RED FOX

"Where are you going, Pat?" asked the cat.
"Shopping," said Pat.
"What are you going to buy, Pat?"

"Dog biscuits," said Pat.

"While you're there, Pat," said the cat, "would you mind getting me a nice piece of fish?"

"Not at all," said Pat.

"Where are you going, Pat?" asked the squirrel.
"Shopping," said Pat.
"What are you going to buy, Pat?"

"Dog biscuits and a nice piece of fish," said Pat.

"Pat, old chap," said the squirrel, "be a good fellow and pop in a packet of peanuts for me, would you?"

"OK," said Pat.

"Where are you going, Pat?" asked the duck.
"Shopping," said Pat.
"What are you going to buy, Pat?"

"Dog biscuits, a nice piece of fish and a packet of peanuts," said Pat.

"Do me a favour, Pat," said the duck. "Bring me back a loaf of bread, if it's no trouble."

"No trouble," said Pat.

"Where are you going, Pat?" asked the hen.
"Shopping," said Pat.
"What are you going to buy, Pat?"

"Dog biscuits, a nice piece of fish, a packet of peanuts and a loaf of bread," said Pat.

"Be an angel, Pat," said the hen, "and get me half a dozen eggs, would you dear? There's a love."

"Of course," said Pat.

"Where are you going, Pat?" asked the pig.
"Shopping," said Pat.
"What are you going to buy, Pat?"

"Dog biscuits, a nice piece of fish, a packet of peanuts, a loaf of bread and half a dozen eggs," said Pat.

"Save me a trip, Pat," said the pig. "I'm halfway through the wash and I'm right out of powder. Could you get me a box? Best make it a large one."

"I'll see what I can do," said Pat.

"Where are you going, Pat?" asked the goat.
"Shopping," said Pat.
"What are you going to buy, Pat?"

"Dog biscuits, a nice piece of fish, a packet of peanuts, a loaf of bread, half a dozen eggs and a box of washing powder, large," said Pat.

"I'd go myself, Pat," said the goat, "but I don't like to leave the kids. Could you get me something for their tea? They'll eat anything."

"Leave it to me," said Pat.

"Phew!" said Pat, "I'll be glad to get home."

"Thanks, Pat," said the goat. "I'm very grateful."

"You're welcome," said Pat.

"Well done, Pat," said the pig. "You've saved my bacon."

"Ho ho," said Pat.

"Thank you, Pat," said the hen. "You're a treasure."

"Don't mention it," said Pat.

"Good old Pat," said the duck. "What would we do without you?"

"It was nothing," said Pat.

"Pat," said the squirrel. "You're a perfect poppet."

"Don't be silly," said Pat.

"Thanks, Pat," said the cat. "You're very kind."

"Not at all," said Pat. "I was going anyway."

"Oh no!" said Pat.

"Where are you going, Pat?" asked the cat.
"Shopping," said Pat.

"What are you going to buy, Pat?"

"Dog biscuits," said Pat.

Some bestselling Red Fox picture books

THE BIG ALFIE AND ANNIE ROSE STORYBOOK
by Shirley Hughes
OLD BEAR
by Jane Hissey
OI! GET OFF OUR TRAIN
by John Burningham
DON'T DO THAT!
by Tony Ross
NOT NOW, BERNARD
by David McKee
ALL JOIN IN
by Quentin Blake
THE WHALES' SONG
by Gary Blythe and Dyan Sheldon
JESUS' CHRISTMAS PARTY
by Nicholas Allan
THE PATCHWORK CAT
by Nicola Bayley and William Mayne
WILLY AND HUGH
by Anthony Browne
THE WINTER HEDGEHOG
by Ann and Reg Cartwright
A DARK, DARK TALE
by Ruth Brown
HARRY, THE DIRTY DOG
by Gene Zion and Margaret Bloy Graham
DR XARGLE'S BOOK OF EARTHLETS
by Jeanne Willis and Tony Ross
WHERE'S THE BABY?
by Pat Hutchins